THE WOMAN IN WHITE

WILKIE COLLINS

www.realreads.co.uk

Retold by Tony Evans
Illustrated by Felix Bennett

Published by Real Reads Ltd
Stroud, Gloucestershire, UK
www.realreads.co.uk

First published in 2011

ISBN 978-1-906230-50-0

Printed in Singapore by Imago Ltd
Designed by Lucy Guenot
Typeset by Bookcraft Ltd, Stroud, Gloucestershire

CONTENTS

The Characters   4

The Woman in White   7

Taking things further   55

THE CHARACTERS

Walter Hartright

Walter is a clever and determined young painting and drawing teacher. Can he solve the puzzle of the woman in white before it is too late?

Laura Fairlie

Laura is delicate and beautiful. Can she escape from the danger which threatens her? Will she ever be able to marry the man she loves?

Marian Halcombe

Laura's half-sister, Marian is a brave and determined young woman. When Laura is in trouble, will she be able to protect her?

4

The Woman in White

Who is the mysterious woman in white, and where does she come from? She looks very like Laura Fairlie – is there some connection between them? Why is she so anxious and afraid?

Sir Percival Glyde

When Sir Percival meets Laura, he does everything he can to please her. Can she really trust him? What secret is he hiding from the world?

Count Fosco

The count is polite and helpful to everyone. Is he Marian's and Laura's friend, or their enemy? What lies beneath his sinister charm?

Mr Frederick Fairlie

Mr Fairlie is Laura's and Marian's uncle. He is a selfish, fussy man who thinks only of his own comfort and convenience.

THE WOMAN IN WHITE

Walter Hartright could hardly believe his
luck. He was a young painting and drawing
teacher, and had just been offered an excellent
job for the next four months, in Cumberland!
When Walter had heard the good news, he
had hurried to tell his mother, who lived a
few miles away from his lodgings in London.
As he walked back home from her cottage
along the gloomy road, his mind was filled
with thoughts about his new job. He would be
teaching two young ladies to paint in water-
colours. Would he enjoy living at Limmeridge
House?

Suddenly, Walter felt the touch of a hand
laid lightly on his shoulder from behind. He
spun round, his fingers gripping his walking
stick. A strange figure stood in front of him,
but he soon realised that he was not in any

danger. It was a young woman, not much more than twenty years old, dressed from head to foot in white clothing. The moonlight showed her pale, youthful face and slender figure. She looked tired and worried, as if she had been walking for miles.

'I am sorry to trouble you,' she said. 'Can you tell me if this is the way to London?'

'You are on the right road, but it is a long way to walk,' Walter replied.

Her hand tightened round his arm. 'I am frightened,' she said. 'Please help me. Is there a carriage I can get?'

At that moment, an empty cab approached from behind, and she hurried towards it. 'I have enough money for my fare. Promise me that if anyone enquires about me, you will say nothing.'

'Very well, if that is your wish, I will tell no one.' Walter helped her into the cab.

'Do you live in London?' she asked.

'Only until tomorrow,' he replied. 'Then I am going north – to Cumberland.'

'Cumberland!' she repeated, her face suddenly smiling. 'I lived there once, and was very happy. If only I could see kind Mrs Fairlie again, and her little daughter Laura – and Limmeridge House.'

When the mysterious woman had left, Walter stood in the middle of the road, amazed. Limmeridge, the home of his new employer! What a peculiar coincidence! A moment later, he heard the sound of galloping horses, and another cab drove past him towards London, then stopped.

A man leant out of the window. 'Have you seen a young woman pass this way?' he asked. 'A woman dressed all in white?'

'No, Sir,' Walter replied, remembering his promise. 'The road has been empty. But why are you looking for her?'

As the cab drove off, the passenger called

out to Walter. 'She has escaped!' he cried. 'The woman in white – she is a mad woman, and she has escaped from my Asylum!'

Two days later, Walter arrived at Limmeridge House, the home of his employer, Mr Frederick Fairlie. The large and pleasant house was set in attractive gardens, close to the sea shore. The day was sunny, and the distant coast of Scotland could be seen through a blue haze on the horizon. He was met by

Miss Marian Halcombe, one of the two young ladies he would be teaching. Marian, twenty-four years old with dark hair and eyes and a confident manner, welcomed him to Limmeridge House.

'My sister, Miss Laura Fairlie, is in the garden,' she told him. 'Let me take you to meet her. We call ourselves sisters, but of course, she is really my half-sister. My father was our mother's first husband, Mr Halcombe. After Mr Halcombe died, our mother remarried – to Mr Philip Fairlie, Laura's father.'

Walter paused. 'First, Miss Halcombe, I need to speak to you about a very strange adventure I had just before my journey to Cumberland.'

Marian asked Walter to sit down, and he told her all about his meeting with the woman in white, and how she had spoken about 'kind Mrs Fairlie and her little daughter Laura.'

Marian looked puzzled. 'Perhaps the woman you met knew Laura when they were both children. I will see what I can find out – some of our mother's old letters might contain a clue. Now let us go into the garden and find Miss Fairlie.'

As Walter followed Marian across the large lawn to the back of the house, he caught his first glimpse of Laura, standing near a wooden table and turning over the pages of a sketch-book that lay at her side. She was twenty years old, a fair, delicate girl with glossy light-brown hair, plainly parted and drawn back over her ears. Something about her appearance made Walter think that he had met her before – but no, that was impossible.

'Look here, Mr Hartright,' Marian said, pointing to Laura's sketch-book. 'Laura must be a very keen pupil. The moment you arrive at the house, she begins to study!'

Laura laughed. 'I am sure that Mr Hartright will not agree with you when he sees my poor sketches!' Walter gazed at her green-blue eyes and smiling face, and felt that he was a very lucky man to be staying at Limmeridge House.

Marian Halcombe soon discovered the connection between the mysterious woman in white and Limmeridge House. Some of her mother's old letters mentioned a young girl, Anne Catherick, who had visited Limmeridge for a few months about eleven years ago, and become friendly with Laura. She and her mother, Mrs Catherick, came from Welmingham near London. It seemed that

Anne had been an unusual child. Although she was intelligent and friendly, she had often acted strangely and had done peculiar things. For example, after Mrs Fairlie once told her she looked pretty dressed in white, she said that she would wear no other colour for as long as she lived. Mrs Fairlie had also mentioned that Anne and Laura looked very much like each other. Walter realised that when he had first seen Laura, it was the mysterious woman in white that she had reminded him of. Of course Laura looked much healthier and happier – but apart from that, the two young women were indeed remarkably similar. Walter wondered why Anne had been put in an Asylum, and hoped that she had managed to reach London safely.

Walter was very happy at Limmeridge. During the day he would go into the garden or to the nearby coast with the young ladies to sketch and paint. In the evening, after dinner with Uncle Frederick, Laura would play the

piano and sing. Walter felt that he had never met such a delightful and attractive young woman. He realised that he was falling in love with Laura.

One evening, after Laura had gone to bed early with a headache, Marian sat next to Walter.

'Mr Hartright,' she said, 'I need to speak seriously to you. I know that you have never said anything to Laura about your feelings for her, but they are very clear to me. I am afraid that you need to forget all about your love for

Laura. She is engaged to be married.'

Walter could not believe it. 'If that is true, why has she never mentioned it?' he asked.

Marian looked anxious. 'The engagement is the result of a promise that Laura made to her father, two years ago. It was his dying wish. Her fiancé, Sir Percival Glyde, is forty-five years old, and is not really the kind of man she would like to marry. However, she feels that it is her duty to agree to her father's wishes. Walter, you need to know that Sir Percival Glyde is coming to Limmeridge the day after tomorrow, to see Laura and fix the date for their wedding. It will be held in Old Welmingham Church, near Blackwater Park, where Sir Percival's parents were married. He wishes the marriage to take place before the end of next month!'

Feeling shocked and upset, Walter decided that he could no longer remain at Limmeridge House. Seeing Sir Percival Glyde and Laura together would be horrible. He spoke to

Frederick Fairlie that evening and pretended that he had received some bad news from London, and would need to return home.

In the morning Walter packed up his belongings, and went down to breakfast. Marian met him as he entered the dining room.

'Laura has received a very upsetting letter,' she said. 'It is from the woman in white – Anne Catherick! Anne has warned Laura against marrying Sir Percival Glyde, but gives no reasons. One of the servants has told me that Anne is staying just a few miles away, at Todd's farm. She knows the family there from when she last lived in Limmeridge. Walter, could you speak with her? I have no one else to ask.'

Walter agreed, and set off for Todd's farm. The road went past the church graveyard, where Laura's and Marian's mother – Mrs

Fairlie – was buried. Suddenly, through the early morning mist, Walter caught a glimpse of a strange, thin woman, wearing a long dark-blue cloak, with the hood drawn over her head. A few inches of her gown were visible below the cloak. Walter's heart beat fast as he noticed the colour – it was white.

She pulled back her hood. It was the woman in white, standing next to Mrs Fairlie's grave!

'You are Walter Hartright, the drawing master,' she said. 'You were kind to me once. Please tell Miss Laura Fairlie that I know Sir Percival Glyde will never make her happy. He is not the man he pretends to be. Now that I have visited dear Mrs Fairlie's grave, I am leaving Todd's farm and returning to London – it is dangerous for me here.'

She would say no more, and Walter watched as she picked her way through the graveyard and disappeared into the mist.

Walter returned to Limmeridge House and told Laura and Marian all that had happened. As he had guessed, it made no difference to Laura's decision.

'I have no reason to doubt Sir Percival's good character,' she said. 'The woman in white cannot persuade me to go against my father's dying wish.'

That afternoon Walter left Limmeridge for ever, determined to find some work in a foreign land where he could try to forget about the past.

The very next day, Sir Percival Glyde arrived at Limmeridge House. He looked rather older than Marian remembered. His head was bald over the forehead, and his face was marked and worn. He treated Laura with politeness and respect, but Marian noticed that Laura looked uneasy and embarrassed when Sir Percival spoke to her. Either he did not notice Laura's dislike of him, or had decided to ignore it.

A few days later the family solicitor arrived. Mr Gilmore was there to discuss Laura's marriage settlement. He spoke a few words in private to Marian.

'Miss Halcome, I am surprised and worried. As you know, Laura Fairlie has a large fortune of £20,000, and I would like her to make a will when she is married, leaving the money to whoever she wishes. But Sir Percival Glyde insists that the marriage settlement should say that if Lady Glyde – Laura – dies before he does, all her money must go straight to him! Surely Laura will now change her mind about the wedding.'

Marian told Laura what Mr Gilmore had said, but Laura was determined to go ahead with the marriage.

'I gave my word to my poor father that I would be Sir Percival's wife,' she said. 'I cannot break that promise. Marian, please tell me that you will visit us at Blackwater Park as soon as we get home from our honeymoon. I have one other thing to ask. Here is a book of Walter Hartright's sketches. There is a lock of my hair inside it. If I were to die before dear Walter, give it to him, and say that I loved him.'

Six months after Laura Fairlie's marriage to Sir Percival Glyde, Marian Halcombe was waiting at Blackwater Park for her half-sister's return from her wedding trip. How strange to think that Laura was now Lady Glyde!

Everything about Blackwater Park made Marian long to be back at Limmeridge House. The ancient building was half-ruined, gloomy and dismal, and full of damp and decay. Outside, an overgrown garden led to Blackwater Lake, dark and stagnant, the sluggish, shallow water looking evil and poisonous.

When Laura arrived at her new home she said little about her husband. Marian wondered if she was already regretting her marriage to Sir Percival.

Sir Percival had brought a close friend back to England to stay at Limmeridge. Count Fosco, who was an Italian nobleman, and his wife the Countess, planned to stay in England for some time. The Countess was a quiet, shy woman, but Fosco was one of the most unusual men Marian had ever met. She found it hard to decide whether she admired him, or was frightened of him. He was immensely fat, but his movements were astonishingly light and easy. His large, pale face was closely shaven all over, and completely free from any marks or wrinkles, although he was almost sixty years old. Marian thought that his thick, dark brown hair was probably a wig. She was fascinated by the extraordinary power of Fosco's eyes, which had a cold, clear glitter in them.

Fosco was always perfectly good-mannered, friendly and helpful, but Marian could see that Laura did not like the Count. Even Sir Percival seemed rather afraid of him.

One morning Sir Percival called Laura and Marian to the library after breakfast. He insisted that Laura should sign a document that he had put on the table in front of her, and that Marian should witness it. When Laura wanted to read the document before she signed, Sir Percival shouted at her in a violent temper. At that point Count Fosco entered the room, and spoke quietly to Sir Percival, who said no more to Laura about the document. Her husband left the room, his face red with anger.

That evening, just before dinner, when Laura and Marian were in Laura's sitting room, there was a tap on the door. It was Count Fosco.

'I will not come in,' he said. 'But I have a suggestion to make. My dear Lady Glyde, your position in this house has become very unpleasant. Write to your guardian, Mr Frederick Fairlie. Give me the letter and I will post it myself. Tell Mr Fairlie that you intend to return to Limmeridge for a short visit – a month or two – without your husband. I will speak to Sir Percival, and make sure that he agrees.'

Laura agreed to do as the Count suggested. She hurriedly wrote the letter and passed it to the Count. However, Marian was suspicious of Fosco. She would go with Laura to Limmeridge House in order to make sure she arrived safely.

After dinner that evening Laura felt tired and went straight to bed. Marian decided to go to the library, but just as she reached the door, she overheard Sir Percival and the Count talking.

'If Lady Glyde refuses to sign the document that will give me her £20,000, I am a ruined man!' Sir Percival cried. There is only one way I can get her money – if she is dead!'

Marian was horrified. She would need all her intelligence and courage to protect her half-sister.

The next day Marian woke up feeling tired and ill. Her head was throbbing violently. Could something in her meal have made her ill, she wondered? When Marian stood up to get dressed, the room seemed to spin around her, and she collapsed back onto the bed.

It was three days before Marian felt well enough to get up. The housekeeper, Mrs Michelson, brought her breakfast in her room.

'Miss Halcombe, I am afraid I have some distressing news for you,' Mrs Michelson said. 'The day after you were taken ill, Lady Glyde left Blackwater Park, intending to go to Limmeridge House. She went first to London, with Count Fosco and his wife, to stay in their house overnight before travelling to Cumberland. Sir Percival left the house shortly afterwards. Last night I received a letter from Countess Fosco. She told me that Lady Glyde had become very ill as soon as she had reached London. A doctor was called, but it was too late. Madam, I am afraid that Lady Glyde has died.'

Marian was deeply shocked by the news. What could have caused such a sudden illness? She decided that she would write to Mr Gilmore, Laura's solicitor, asking him to find out exactly what had happened. She would ask Mr Gilmore to post his reply to Limmeridge House, where she would be going for Laura's funeral. She did not have Walter Hartridge's address in America, so she wrote to Mrs Hartridge, Walter's mother, telling her about Laura.

Laura's body was taken from London to Limmeridge by Count Fosco. On the day of the funeral, Marian received a reply from Mr Gilmore. He had obtained a copy of the death certificate, signed by a qualified doctor, which said that Lady Glyde had died from a serious, long-term heart condition. It seemed that Laura must have had heart disease for years without realising it. Mr Gilmore could find nothing suspicious about her death.

After the funeral, Count Fosco asked if he could speak to Marian and her uncle about some important news.

'My dear Mr Fairlie – my dear Miss Halcombe. I have received some information from Sir Percival Glyde which I must pass on to you – a thousand pardons for troubling you at this distressing time. Mrs Catherick's daughter, Anne, has been found. She has been safely returned to the Asylum from which she escaped.'

'The woman in white!' cried Marian.

'Indeed,' Fosco replied. 'The poor young woman will be well looked after. Unfortunately, while she has been away from the Asylum, her peculiar state of mind has got worse. She now believes that she is not Anne Catherick at all – she is absolutely convinced that she is Lady Glyde! Of course there was some resemblance between the poor woman and the late Lady Glyde, which has probably brought on this delusion. I have mentioned this because it is possible that Anne may write to you or Mr Fairlie about her foolish claim.'

Frederick Fairlie nodded. 'Thank you for warning us, Count Fosco. Let us hope she causes us no trouble.'

Marian was silent. Could there be some other reason why Anne was pretending to be Laura? Marian decided that as soon as she left Limmeridge, she would visit the Asylum and speak to Anne Catherick herself. It was a great pity that Walter Hartright was not in England to help her. Poor Walter – he would be heartbroken when he heard the news about Laura's death.

Just as Marian was leaving Cumbria and
returning to seek out Anne Catherick, Walter
Hartridge was stepping ashore in London. The
first thing he did was to visit his mother to
let her know he had returned safely from his
travels, and to ask for any news of Laura. It was
from her that he heard that Laura had died.
Walter promised himself that as soon as he
possibly could, he would travel to Limmeridge
to visit Laura's grave and say his goodbyes. He
found it hard to believe that he would never
again see the woman he loved.

It did not take Marian Halcombe long to find out to which Asylum Anne Catherick had been sent. It was close to Blackwater Park, and near Welmingham, where Mrs Catherick lived. When Marian told the manager that she was Frederick Fairlie's niece, she was allowed to meet Anne, who was walking in the gardens with a nurse close by.

Marian saw two women walking along a gravel path. As soon as she was within a dozen paces of them, one of the women stopped for an instant, shook off the nurse's grasp, and rushed into Marian's arms. At that moment, Marian recognised her half-sister – it was Laura, not Anne Catherick! She was alive!

After she had recovered from the shock, Marian thought very quickly. She told Laura that she would return to help her escape, but made her promise to say nothing about their meeting to anyone. Marian gave the nurse some money and persuaded her to tell no one what had happened. She arranged to meet the nurse outside the Asylum at five o'clock the next day.

Before her next meeting with the nurse, Marian went to her bank in London and drew out all the money she had in the world. Half of it was enough to persuade the nurse to let Laura escape, and soon Laura and Marian were on the train back to Limmeridge. Laura looked older, thinner and more troubled than the last time she had been at Limmeridge – but surely, Marian thought, Mr Fairlie could not fail to recognise his niece.

During the journey to Cumbria, Laura explained to Marian what had happened to her after she had left Blackwater Park with Count Fosco and his wife. When they had arrived at

Fosco's London house, Laura had been offered a cup of tea. She remembered that it had tasted very strange, and made her feel faint and dizzy – and the next thing she knew, she was in a carriage, dressed all in white, with a stern-faced nurse at her side. She was taken to the Asylum, where everyone called her Anne Catherick.

'I told them that there had been a terrible mistake, and that I was Lady Laura Glyde, but no-one listened to me,' Laura said.

As Laura spoke, Marian could see that Laura had been very badly affected by her terrible experience. She seemed very tired and nervous. She could remember being taken to the Asylum, but her memory of everything that had happened *before* she had arrived at Fosco's London house was very poor. Laura seemed to have forgotten nearly everything about her life at Limmeridge House before she was married.

As soon as Marian and Laura arrived at Limmeridge House, they were shown straight to Mr Fairlie. When he saw how much Laura's appearance had changed, and when she seemed unable to answer simple questions about Limmeridge and her family, he refused to believe her story.

'You have been tricked by that mad woman,' he said to Marian. 'Anyone can see that this person is Anne Catherick, not Lady Glyde! We must make arrangements for her return to the Asylum.'

Marian saw that it would be dangerous for them to stay in Limmeridge, and after telling Mr Fairlie that they would wait for him, Marian and Laura set off back to the railway station. They

would have to return to London. On the way,
Laura said that if she was to leave Limmeridge
for ever, she would like to visit her mother's
grave for the last time. Marian agreed, and
the two women walked into the graveyard and
towards the marble stone where Mrs Fairlie
had been buried. The same stone now had
another inscription, recording the death of
Lady Glyde, but the two women knew that
whoever lay buried there, it was not Laura. As
they approached the grave, they saw a young
man walking towards it from the opposite
direction. He came closer, looked at them, then
staggered back in amazement.

'Laura!' he cried. 'Can it really be you?'

'Yes, Walter,' Laura replied. 'It is really me. And you have come back to me at last!'

Walter was overjoyed to find that Laura was still alive. Marian soon told him everything that had happened since he had gone to America.

'The three of us must return to London,' Walter said. 'We will find lodgings in a quiet part of the city where Sir Percival and Count Fosco will not be able to discover us. I have some savings, and Marian still has some of the money she took out of the bank. When we have found a new home, I will try to find a way to prove that Laura is telling the truth. The police and law courts cannot help us until we find some evidence against Sir Percival Glyde and Count Fosco.'

Soon afterwards Walter, Laura and Marian were safely settled in London, where no one would recognise them. Walter decided that he would start his investigations by going to Welmingham and meeting with Mrs Catherick, Anne's mother. The first thing Walter asked about was the strange resemblance between Anne and Laura.

'You may as well know the truth,' Mrs Catherick said. 'I met Philip Fairlie – Laura's father – when he was a single man, the year before his marriage to Laura's mother. We had a child. Philip is Anne's real father. I did not marry Philip, but later, when I married Mr Catherick, we brought Anne up as our own daughter. Of course, Mrs Fairlie never knew.'

'So Anne and Laura have the same father – no wonder they look so alike!'

'Just so. But Anne was always a strange child, and behaved in peculiar ways. When we stayed in Limmeridge for a while, she got an idea in her head about always wearing white, and has done so ever since. Many years ago, I discovered something about Sir Percival Glyde which would ruin him if it became known. He paid me money to keep quiet about it. One day, I was foolish enough to tell Anne that I knew a secret about Sir Percival. I did not tell her what the secret was about – but the silly girl went round telling people she knew something, and eventually Sir Percival found out. He was convinced that Anne knew all about his secret, and forced me to put her in an Asylum, to keep her quiet. She has hated Sir Percival ever since, and thinks he is a wicked man – that is why she tried to stop Laura Fairlie marrying him. She managed to escape, but was captured again by Sir Percival and Count Fosco.'

'And Sir Percival Glyde's secret?' Walter asked. 'Are you able to say what it is?'

Mrs Catherick looked frightened. 'All I

can tell you is that it concerns Sir Percival's
parents,' she said. 'Please do not ask me to
reveal any more.'

After his meeting with Mrs Catherick, Walter
thought long and hard about what she had
said to him. He decided he would visit Old
Welmingham Church, near Blackwater Park,
where Sir Percival Glyde's parents had been
married. He would examine the marriage
records kept in the church vestry, to see if he
could find any clue to Sir Percival's secret.

After Walter arrived at Old Welmingham, he got the keys to the church vestry from the parish clerk, who lived nearby. He soon found the entry he was looking for. Walter was disappointed. It seemed a perfectly ordinary record of the marriage between Sir Felix Glyde and his bride, Cecilia Jane Elster – Sir Percival's parents. Then Walter noticed that the entry had been squeezed into a small space at the bottom of the page. When the parish clerk told Walter that a second copy of the marriage register was kept in the clerk's house, Walter asked if he could see it, to check the entry.

The clerk went home and brought the copy to the vestry. Walter took the dusty, leather-bound volume over to a desk in the corner. He found the record of the marriage before Sir Felix Glyde's, and the marriage after it – but in between there was nothing! This was Sir Percival Glyde's secret. Although his mother and father were always believed to be married, no wedding ceremony had ever taken place, and therefore 'Sir' Percival had no legal right to inherit his father's title, or the Blackwater Park Estate.

It was clear to Walter what must have happened. Sir Percival had altered the marriage register kept in the church vestry, not realising that a second copy was kept by the clerk. When Sir Percival thought Anne knew his secret, he had to keep her quiet. Walter knew that Anne had never returned to the Asylum – Laura had been sent in her place. So where was Anne now, Walter wondered – could her body have been the one that the doctor examined in Count Fosco's house?

The next afternoon, Walter returned to London. When he reached home, Marian and Laura met him on the doorstep. They looked very serious.

'We have just received some important news from Mr Gilmore,' Marian said. 'Sir Percival Glyde is dead. Mr Gilmore said that for some reason, Sir Percival had visited the vestry at Old Welmingham Church late last night, carrying an oil lamp. Some of the old papers in the vestry must have caught fire, and Sir Percival found himself trapped inside.'

Walter thought quickly. Perhaps Sir Percival had found out about his visit to the church, and had been trying to destroy the evidence of the forgery – at any rate, it had done him no good. He had paid for his crimes.

'We still need to find out what happened to Anne Catherick,' he said. 'I have decided to see Count Fosco. I will give him a choice. If he writes a signed confession, I will let him escape to Italy. If he refuses, I will hand him over to the police. I feel sure that Fosco will not want them to investigate his part in the plot to kidnap Laura.'

That evening, Walter visited Fosco's house. When he heard about what Walter had already discovered, he agreed to tell the truth in order to escape justice.

'Sir Percival was badly in debt, and desperate to get his wife's £20,000,' Fosco said. 'Because I knew his secret – that his

parents were not married, and that he should not
have inherited his title or his estate – some of this
money was promised to me. When we tracked
down Anne Catherick, she became very ill, and
we found out that she had severe heart disease.
That was when we worked out a plan to solve all
our problems. Sir Percival still believed that Anne
knew all about his secret, so we decided to keep
her prisoner in London until she died. Because
the two women looked very similar, we could
pretend her dead body was Lady Laura Glyde, and
get a death certificate, so that Sir Percival could
inherit Lady Glyde's fortune.

'And you got the real Lady Glyde out of the way by putting her in the Asylum, making everyone think she was poor Anne!' Walter said. 'But what if Anne had lived another few weeks? How could you have been sure that she died in time to get the death certificate for Lady Glyde?'

Fosco smiled. 'My dear Mr Hartright, rest assured that she would have died in time. I would have made certain of it. Now, please allow me to write my confession for you. I wish to leave for Italy as soon as possible.'

Walter, Marian and Laura left London for Limmeridge House the next day. At first Laura's uncle refused to see her – he said it would be too much trouble for him. Then Walter showed him Fosco's signed confession. Faced with this, Mr Fairlie was forced to agree that Laura really was his niece, and all his servants and neighbours were told the good news. Laura was pleased that she was recognised by everyone again, but she was so upset by her uncle's selfish attitude, that she did not want to stay in Limmeridge House.

'We will never see your £20,000 again,' Walter said. 'The money was all used to pay Sir Percival's debts, and to pay Count Fosco. But you are safe and well, which is all that matters to me. I will be able to earn enough for both of us. We will return to London, and of course Marian must come with us too.'

Five months later, Walter and Laura were married. The following year their first son – also called Walter – was born. One day Laura was sitting in their garden with her baby boy by her side. Marian sat next to her. Suddenly Walter came rushing down the path. He was waving a letter.

'We have had a great deal of news from Mr Gilmore. First, Laura, I am sorry to say that your uncle, Mr Frederick Fairlie, died last week. But do you know who Mr Gilmore says will inherit Limmeridge House, and the whole Limmeridge estate? He tells us that it is our son, little Walter!'

Laura was sad to hear of her uncle's death, but was pleased that her son's future was secure. It also meant that they would return to the house that held many happy memories for her.

'And what is his other news?' Marian asked.

Walter frowned. 'It is about Count Fosco. It seems that the Count has been found dead – murdered. Mr Gilmore believes that he was involved with some kind of secret society. I cannot say that the news upsets me. Count Fosco, like Sir Percival Glyde, has finally paid for his sins and can trouble us no more. Now, let us get ready to travel to Cumbria.'

Walter picked up his son, and held him high in the air. 'This important young gentleman, the new Master of Limmeridge, must return to claim his inheritance!'

TAKING THINGS FURTHER

The real read

This *Real Reads* version of *The Woman in White* is a retelling of Wilkie Collins' famous original work. If you would like to read the full story, many complete editions are available, from bargain paperbacks to beautiful hardbacks. You should be able to find a copy in your local library, book shop or charity shop.

Filling in the spaces

The loss of so many of Wilkie Collins' original words is a sad but necessary part of the shortening process. We have had to make some difficult decisions, omitting subplots and details, some important, some less so, but all interesting. We have also, at times, taken the liberty of combining two events into one, or of giving a character words or actions that originally belong to another. The points below will fill in some of the gaps, but nothing can beat the original.

- The original story is told by nine different people, including Walter Hartright and Marian Halcombe. Each person describes what happens from their point of view.

- Before Laura gets married, Mr Gilmore investigates Sir Percival Glyde but can find no evidence against him. When Laura goes to Blackwater Park after her marriage, Anne Catherick meets her there, but she is recaptured by Count Fosco.

- Laura's financial affairs are more complicated than in this version. As well as having £20,000 which Sir Percival plans to inherit, she has another £10,000 which would go to her aunt if Laura died. Her aunt is married to Count Fosco, so both Fosco and Sir Percival would benefit from her death.

- We are told more about the time that Walter spends abroad. He goes to Honduras, in Central America, and has some dangerous and exciting adventures.

- More details are given about Mrs Catherick, Anne's mother. Mrs Catherick treats Anne badly, and Anne is cared for by a kind neighbour, Mrs Clements. We learn that many years ago Mrs Catherick helped Sir Percival Glyde forge the marriage entry in the church register, and that since then he has paid her to keep his secret.

- When Walter is investigating the marriage of Sir Percival's parents, he has to fight off some men hired by Sir Percival, who attack him.

- In the original story, the date of Laura's false death certificate is an important clue. Walter is able to prove that Laura was taken to Count Fosco's house on the day after the death certificate was signed, showing that the dead person could not possibly have been Laura.

Back in time

Many of the buildings and other landmarks constructed in Victorian times are still very much a part of modern-day life. For example, nearly all our railway lines and many of our churches and town halls were built during the reign of Queen Victoria, between 1837 and 1901. Other things, however, have now disappeared, including the Victorian 'lunatic asylums' for people who were thought to have mental illness. These were very large buildings, usually built in open countryside and surrounded by high railings so that no one could escape. They were like separate worlds, often with their own bakery, laundry, farm and gardens. Each asylum contained hundreds of patients. Many of them, like Anne Catherick – the woman in white – did not need to be shut away from the outside world. The Victorians had a poor understanding of mental illness, and the asylums held lots of people who had learning difficulties, or who were anxious or physically ill. Nearly all the old asylum buildings have now been demolished or put to other uses, and today patients who need help will instead go to their doctor's surgery, or local hospital.

Another difference between mid-Victorian Britain and life today was the position of women, particularly married women. After Laura Fairlie marries Sir Percival Glyde she is very much in his power, and can do little to prevent his bad treatment of her. Until a law was passed in 1882 – The Married Women's Property Act – a woman's money was owned by her husband when she got married. As Laura married Sir Percival in 1850, this means that Sir Percival did not really need to try to force her to sign the document giving him her £20,000 – it already belonged to him! We don't know if Wilkie Collins made a mistake when he wrote this part of the story, or if he intended Sir Percival Glyde to be ignorant of the law.

Finding out more

We recommend the following books and websites to gain a greater understanding of Wilkie Collins and the world he lived in.

Books

- Andrew Gasson, *Wilkie Collins: An Illustrated Guide*, OUP, 1998.

- Liz Gogerly, *The Victorians* (Reconstructed Series), Wayland, 2005.

- Terry Deary, *Vile Victorians* (Horrible Histories), Scholastic, 2007.

- Ann Kramer, *Victorians* (Eyewitness Guides), Dorling Kindersley, 2011.

- Sarah Rutherford, *The Victorian Asylum*, Shire Publications, 2008.

Websites

- www.wilkiecollins.com
Links to free electronic versions of many of Wilkie Collins' books, plus copies of letters, family pictures and lots of other information.

- www.wilkie-collins.info

Information about Wilkie Collins' life and
work, with links to other interesting websites.

- www.victorianweb.org

A good site to find out more about Victorian
times – including writers, other famous people
and everyday life.

- www.bbc.co.uk/history/british/victorians

The BBC's website all about Victorian Britain,
with a wide range of information and activities.

Food for thought

Here are a few things to think about if you are
reading *The Woman in White* alone, or ideas for
discussion if you are reading it with friends.

In retelling *The Woman in White* we have
tried to recreate, as accurately as possible,
Wilkie Collins' original plot and characters.
We have also tried to imitate aspects of his
style. Remember, however, that this is not the
original work; thinking about the points below,
therefore, can help you to begin to understand

Wilkie Collins' craft. To move forward from here, turn to the full-length version of *The Woman in White* and lose yourself in his exciting and imaginative story.

Starting points

● Which character in the story do you find most interesting? Why?

● Do you think Laura was right to keep her promise to her father, and marry Sir Percival Glyde?

● What clues does Wilkie Collins give us to show that Sir Percival Glyde and Count Fosco are unpleasant men?

● How can we tell that Marion Halcombe is a brave and determined woman?

● Was it right for Walter to agree to let Count Fosco go free, if the Count wrote a confession?

Themes

What do you think Wilkie Collins is saying about the following themes in *The Woman in White*?

- love

- marriage

- secrets

- money

- hypocrisy (pretending to be one kind of person, but acting like another)

Style

Can you find paragraphs containing examples of the following?

- vivid descriptions of places or scenery which add to the atmosphere of the story

- descriptions of characters which suggest things about their personality and behaviour

- dramatic scenes which take the reader by surprise

- small details in the story which turn out to be important clues later on

Look closely at how these paragraphs are written. What do you notice? Can you write a paragraph in the same style?